Jordan Tweddle

Pillock

Salamander Street

PLAYS

Cover Photography: Chris Chapman

PB ISBN: 9781068696213

10 9 8 7 6 5 4 3 2 1

Further copies of this publication can be purchased from
www.salamanderstreet.com

Wordville

ACKNOWLEDGEMENTS

A special thank you to Rachael Gill-Davis, Ellie Rose, the staff team at Contact Theatre, Liz Stevenson, Emma Bonnici, Rebecca Clarke, Pip Chapman, Jess Turton, Stewart Campbell all of our Crowdfunder supporters, and my wonderful parents and family.

Pillock previewed at Shakespeare North on the 12th of July 2024, then at Contact Theatre on the 17th and 18th of July, before premiering at Assembly Room as part of the Edinburgh Festival Fringe on the 3rd of August 2024 with Jordan Tweddle in the title role.

CAST

Pillock: **Jordan Tweddle**

CREATIVES

Writer: **Jordan Tweddle**

Director: **Scott Le Crass**

Movement Director: **Kieran Sheehan**

Producer: **Jordan Tweddle / Knock & Nash**

Sound Design: **Pierre Flasse**

Support: **Contact Theatre**

PR: **Chloé Nelkin Consulting**

Dramaturgy: **Lee Mattinson & Scott Le Crass**

Cover Photography: **Chris Chapman**

Cover Artwork: **Jess Reid**

ABOUT THE CAST AND CREATIVES

Jordan Tweddle | Writer, Performer, Producer

Jordan is an award-winning actor, director and writer. He trained at the Manchester School of Theatre, and since graduating has worked across television, film and theatre. He won Best Actor in the 2019 at the Top Indie Film Awards and Monkey Bread Tree Film Awards for his role of Jack in *Don't Blame Jack* as part of Boys on Film 20. His acting credits include: *Coronation Street* (ITV), *Steel* (Theatre by the Lake / National Theatre), *BBC's First Homosexual* (Inkbrew Productions / BBC), *Wings* (Theatre by the Lake), *Frozen* (UK Tour), *Lemons Lemons Lemons Lemons Lemons* (Theatre by the Lake), *Canopy of Stars* (Tristan Bates Theatre) and *Desire Lines* (National Trust).

Scott Le Crass: Director

Scott trained as an actor at Arts Ed and was a director on the Birmingham Rep's first Foundry Programme. In 2022, he completed the National Theatre Director's Course. He is an Associate Director for Pleasure Dome Theatre Company and has directed all of their productions to date including *A Christmas Carol* (Brewhouse, Taunton), *Louisa* (South West Tour) and *A Midsummer Night's Dream* (The Valley of Rocks).

Other credits include: Director—*Rose* (West End), *Cut The Crap* starring Sharon Osbourne (West End), *Jab* (Finborough Theatre), *Jump* (Tour-Qweer Dog Theatre), *Toxic* (HOME, Manchester), *Buff* (Edinburgh Fringe/Plymouth Theatre Royal), *Rose* (Hope Mill Theatre/Park Theatre), *My Dear Aunty Nell* (Tour), *Merboy* (Omnibus Theatre), *Buff, Thirsty* (Vault Festival), *The Railway Children* (OVO Roman Theatre), *Seven Celebrations* (Orange Tree Theatre), *Twelfth Night* (East London Shakespeare Festival), *Elmer* (UK and International Tour/Sell A Door), *Sid* (Arts Theatre and UK Tour), *Country Music* (Omnibus Theatre), *The Witches* (Watford Palace), *Alice in Wonderland* (Old, Rep, Birmingham).

Kieran Sheehan | Movement Director

Kieran is a movement artist working with all kinds of people to develop productions, projects, companies, education and ideas. He has published and presented on intuitive movement and is currently developing artistic projects led with communities. He has worked within theatre, opera, circus, actor training and choreographing his own dance theatre work for the last 20 years. He hopes to remain curious about how artistic and everyday life can become more regularly experienced together, and how this might be a helpful thing to do.

Pierre Flasse | Sound Designer

Pierre Flasse is a composer, sound designer, performer and educator based in Manchester. He fearlessly explores diverse musical landscapes while remaining true to his own voice—whether delving into the realms of spiritual jazz, cinematic music or electronica, his sound pulsates with genuine emotion and raw honesty. He is an avid collaborator and theatre maker, composer's assistant to Sally Potter OBE, and writes for numerous originals projects. His credits include: *The Bell Curves* (Contact, Manchester), *Tales At Twilight* (CAST, Doncaster), *Zugzwang* (Rochdale Town Hall), *Joy Unspeakable* (The Octagon, Bolton), *BIG STRONG MAN* (CAST, Doncaster). He is mentored by sound designer Pete Malkin (*Harry Potter And The Cursed Child, The Encounter, Death of England*).

Knock & Nash Productions | Producer

Founded in 2019, Knock & Nash Productions is a queer and neurodiverse-led production house that commissions and produces fearlessly bold new writing for stage and screen. Knock & Nash champions regional stories with a focus on bringing northern voices to the frontline; creating distinctive and imaginative work with the most talented artists. They also operate an in-house drama school, with a focus on providing accessible actor training to those who may be unable to train otherwise. They operate schools in: Newcastle Upon Tyne, Manchester, Edinburgh, Carlisle and Liverpool. More information at knockandnash.co.uk.

Contact Theatre | Support

Contact Theatre is where audiences come to be curious. Our creative activities are diverse, inspiring and in tune with today. From creating productions to appointing staff and collaborators, we encourage 13 to 30-year-olds to turn the seed of an idea into something spectacular. Positivity and performing arts can change lives. With real investment and the right infrastructure in place, we make this happen every day. Contact is proud to be proof of what can be achieved by putting the future first. Our reputation stretches across Europe and beyond. Most of all, we're proud to be a multi-arts hub for Manchester—and a home for everyone. Whether you're seeking the spotlight or a cosy nook in the cafe, Contact is where everyone comes to be themselves. So come on in, dip a biscuit in your brew and your toes into something new.

Jordan Tweddle

Pillock

CHARACTERS

PILLOCK

EUGENE

NOTES ON THE PLAY

Dialogue in standard font is the voice of Pillock.
Dialogue in **bold** is the voice of Eugene.
Both parts are played by one actor dressed in a double-breasted
navy suit and bleached blonde hair. The actor should be queer and
neurodiverse.

The soundtrack is electronic and should feel like a video game.
The environment of each location is key and should inform
the sound of each space. The scenes should should be heavily
punctuated with a transition sound, think handbrake turns from
moment to moment.

#01 THE MUGGLE JOB

A long sustained beep.

AUTOMATED V/O: Please enter the room.

The overhead light flickers on. They are bright, painfully bright.

They hum.

He sits.

PILLOCK: Adam Barnes.

27.

Date of birth?

18th of September 1996.

I'm not sure what you've got on file

but

Flat 5

Sadlers Tower

Manchester

M14 4QP.

Yes...

erm...

just here for my test results.

Dr Taylor said I should come in.

mmhmm...

yeah...

I think so...

no...

no...

He shakes his head.

I don't drink.

Sorry what did you...?

Family history?

Yeah

my Dad

he's

he's not with us anymore...

It's not your fault...

No

I've already gone through this with Dr Taylor

so could we just...

right...

no...

right...

I understand...

Symptoms?

Neck swelling

weight loss

tired

so fucking tired

like all the fucking time.

So those test results?

I know...

I know...

I know...

I know...

It's just that I...

I'd really like to...

I don't smoke or drink.

I've already told you that.

No, no, no...

Sorry.

I'm sorry...

I don't see what this has to do with anything.

I've already gone over all this.

I'm just here for the test results

So can you just give me the fucking...

I just want...

Please.

I just want the test results.

A pause.

Long uncomfortable silence.

A perfectly timed tear rolls slowly down his cheek.

What?

I'm fine.

I'm fine.

Could you say that again?

Right.

How long?

How long do I have?

So what happens now?

What's the next?

A beep.

AUTOMATED V/O: Move on to the next station.

#02 BALD PERVE

Music booms into the space.

He lights a cigarette.

PILLOCK: What a load of fucking shite.

Y'know 'em minging warning labels you get on ciggie packets?

Well, drama school should come with one of 'em

but, instead of a gammy toeless foot

or some lass coughing up blood

it's just a pic of a middle-class bald perve looking disappointed

as you do Hamlet's fourth soliloquy as an arctic puffin.

Then, when you finally get out

it's endless debt

rejections

(if they can be arsed to send one)

and that looming feeling that no matter what you do

or how hard you work

your life is heading nowhere.

No choice but to take these medical roleplay jobs

giving Oscar-worthy performances for a tenner an hour.

Mind you

leukemia's not that bad.

I had gonorrhoea last week.

They gave me a photo of a manky cock spunking green Mr Whippy

to show for the examination

and somehow I actually managed to convince myself I had it.

My toes go sweaty

they always do that when I feel badly and I fainted

pillock.

I'm crap with puss and blood and shit

not shit like *actual* shit

cos I don't mind a bit of shit

not

not saying I *like* shit or anything

cos like that would be

that's weird.

I mean shit as in other shit like

bodily fluids

phlegm

ear wax

breast milk

How the fuck do you get milk from a tit?

Even the thought makes my toes moist.

Maybe that's why I'm gay.

Men are lovely and dry.

Yeah

gay

faggot

bender.

Haven't heard from my agent

Carl

in a month.

The fucker must be dead.

Last I heard from him was that audition I had for a Weetabix
commercial.

Didn't get it.

Haven't eaten it since.

It's rank anyway

and you can't open a packet without crumbing the entire kitchen

and

I don't own a hoover.

Like, honestly, I'm a slightly above-mediocre actor.

Actor.

If I can even call myself that at the moment.

And it's not like I'm asking for much.

Shop assistant number five.

Homosexual number three.

Corpse number seven.

I'd take out.

Anything to get me away from this fucking

Jay Parker.

By the way

that's my name.

Not Adam.

That must of been confusing.

How do?

Originally from smelly Wigton.

No legit

that's what we call it

cos it stinks.

The Wigton pong

plooming from the cling-film factory

which is definitely having some sort of radioactive effect

cos the local B&M looks like the Monsters Inc cast are on day release.

So I say I'm from the Lake District to make it sound posh

that or

Tebay Services but further up

that really gets people excited.

Fabulous sausage roll.

Moved to the city to find

friends

fame and

feelings.

Yet to find any of 'em.

LOL.

Lactose-intolerant

can't eat a Dairylee Dunkable without shitting my pants.

Never had leukemia or the clap

just to clear that up.

well, maybe the clap once

or twice

but I mean who hasn't?

Single

permanently on my tod

so if you like what you see please feel free to wait behind at the end.

ADHD

chaos somehow always seems to finds me.

Yep. If God were real

right

why did he mess up so bad making me?

Maybe fancied a laugh

maybe I'm heaven's comedy channel

Princess Di and Shirley Bassey up there pissing 'emselves

Is Shirley Bassey even dead?

ADHD.

Already told you that.

Brain works faster than my bowel when I've had a Babybel.

Shit.

Fuck.

Stop.

The music stops.

Sorry.

Pillock.

I've done that thing again.

That thing where I over explain

too many details

a lengthy prologue

but don't worry.

It's under control.

I keep myself sharp by asking questions like

what was I about to do right this second?

I'm a Sim who's actions keep being cancelled.

(*to the gallery*) Oh.

You can restart the music here

if you want

not telling you what to do or owt.

The music kicks back in.

And back.

I'm a Sim who's actions keep being cancelled.

A hop

skip

and a jump

all at once.

Either that or

a sit

start

and where the fuck are my keys?

Mario Kart but you're stuck on a roundabout

no fucking breaks

and the final lap track is playing on loop.

One minute I'm here

the next I'm...

#03 HOME

PILLOCK: Bassenthwaite Lake

standing at the same edge I stood at as a kid.

Mam

and

Dad

ice cream dripping down my fingers

dairy-free cos they actually do that here now

finally keeping up with the times

the post-breakup ice cream binge

raspberry ripple.

#04 HMV

PILLOCK: I fucking love HMV.

I like to own my films in physical form

have 'em in my hands.

I don't need to own every movie

I get that's unreasonable

just the ones

I like to call

shelf-worthy.

The ones I know I'll watch again.

I'm flicking through titles beginning with

F.

Mam calls.

Decline.

That's when I *pillock*
realise I have no idea what I'm looking for anymore
or why I even came in here in the first place
so I stop for a moment to work it out.

He stops for a moment to work it out.

A hand reaches over me
sorry.
The hand grabs summat from the E section.
Eternal Sunshine of the Spotless Mind.
Solid choice.
Joined to the hand is a man
A man with a face
A good face.
The sort of face that looked like people would love.
A person people would want to be.
A bit older than my usual type
but he's a snack.
His real snack equivalent would be a bag of spicy Nik Naks.
He opens his mush and smiles a perfect smile.
Solid gum-to-tooth ratio.
Our eyes meet for a second
maybe
and my brain maps out our entire future.
This feeling fizzes behind my eyes
it's radge
and it's scary and
it's primal.
I would very much like to see his penis.

#05 BRAIN FART

PILLOCK: Do you know on Come Dine with Me

when they ratch through each others drawers

to try and get to know each other better?

Wait

sorry

too soon

pillock.

#06 MUGGLE JOB, TAKE TWO

The lights flicker on.

Painfully bright.

The hum.

PILLOCK: GMC Number 7553419.

Dark hair.

Green eyes.

Honks of tuna.

I switch to mouth breathing which was the worst idea cos I'm
now tasting his stench...

fishy.

Gives smelly Wigton a run for its money.

I've been assigned a cultural competency script

basically

I play a young lad who's just discovered he likes dick

I then score the junior doctors on my homophobe-ometer.

GMC 7553419 begins to spit bars on

moral compasses

HIV

and disappointed parents.

I hear too much of everything except from him

the buzzing of the lights

the cars outside

the actor in the room next door

I think she's got rickets.

My brain is racing

burning through an entire tank of gas

but I'm going nowhere

pedal and brake at the same time

then I'm thinking about HMV guy

the one with the face and

the solid gum-to-tooth ratio

and I suddenly want to to know every single possible thing
about him

not just like all the impressive shit but like all the boring shit
too

like

can he handle extra hot at Nandos?

Twiglets

yay or nay?

And what's his favourite episode of Schitt's Creek?

AUTOMATED V/O: Move on to the next station.

PILLOCK: I fail GMC 7553419

and add poor personal hygiene to the notes.

#07 GHOSTS AND COUPLES, COUPLES AND GHOSTS

PILLOCK: Gay dating is basically being ghosted

and

accidentally

swiping right on couples.

Went on two good dates with a guy

well, at least I thought they were good

a fellow thespian

shady bastards the lot of us.

He said we had different communication styles

and then blocked me.

No explanation.

Finito.

Poof.

Houdini.

Like it never really happened.

But

I can handle rejection.

I'm an actor.

Used to it.

I can handle rejection really well.

#08 BUSSY

Nightclub.

PILLOCK is cabbaged.

PILLOCK: On to the next

that's what we say in the biz

on to the fucking next

a different direction

it didn't go my way this time and that's fine

I'll find summat a little more right

A better fit

my big break is coming

oh boy is it coming.

I wap out the app to find my next big break

my future opportunity

my onwards and upwards

unlimited access to other

horny

lonely

people

ranked in order of distance

A sat-nav for shagging

I scroll through faces of failed talking stages

headless torsos

and the lad I rimmed in the back of his Corsa.

I can't see HMV guy on here.

Must be straight.

At home with some bombshell watching his copy of Eternal
Sunshine.

New message.

Ariana Grindr.

54 metres away.

Asks me to fuck his bussy

(whatever that actually is)

and to meet him in the cubicle upstairs

no hello or nothing

straight to the down and dirty.

Probably not my cup of tea.

Probably doesn't float my boat.

Probably ain't my bag.

#09 ARIANA GRINDR

PILLOCK: I'm in the cubicle.

Absolutely cabbaged.

The reckless party sequence like in Babylon

or Wolf of Wall Street.

Ariana Grindr's sucking me off

on his knees

looking up at me with his pretty Puss in Boots eyes

really going to town like

committed

cupping the balls

the lot.

And whilst that thing he's doing with his tongue feels fucking class

I realise

I'm so fucking lonely

I'm game to let someone do whatever they want to me

so I can feel wanted for a moment

to pretend I'm not alone.

I don't even know his real name.

The cubicle is getting smaller suddenly

can't breathe

trapped

gotta make it quick.

Then I'm thinking of HMV guy again

his mush

his smile

etcher-sketched on the back of my eyelids.

I make noises

pull a few faces

I come

he doesn't.

There's summat thrilling in blowing my load to summat

someone

I can't have.

Ariana Grindr asks if he can snort coke off my dick.

I let him.

Phone rings.

My Mam.

He goes to leave when I ask him a question

do you ever feel like you're drowning?

#10 THE UNIVERSE

PILLOCK: I don't know how much I believe in this Universe

mumbo-jumbo

but I see him again

HMV guy

he doesn't see me like

his back is turned

but I'd recognise that sweet little heinie anywhere.

My adrenaline fires on all cylinders

and I decide to follow him

not in a weird like stalker way

no

but in like an endearing

harmless

romantic lead sorta way

a temporary lapse of judgement fuelled by passionate feelings like in Groundhog Day

yeah

like that.

I see him heading into the

Yoga Loft

(I'd rather put my head in a camel's backside)

but opposites do attract

right?

Google sez when the universe wants bring two people together

it typically creates unavoidable opportunities

and that we shouldn't ignore these opportunities

cos it's trying to align your paths

So maybe this is my shot?

A shot at the sort of love people run through airports for

like in The Wedding Singer

or Love Actually

a love where you get to learn somebody

know somebody

before offering 'em your bussy

(whatever that actually is).

Gotta.

Calm.

Down.

He's straight.

Wasn't on the app.

Gotta remember that if a straight guy is nice to me

doesn't mean he fancies me.

Not falling in love with another straight man.

Not today.

No sire.

But then I see him grab the bannister on the way up the stairs

so he must be bent.

Sometimes my body does the thing where it's in motion

before I can even think about it

cos I'm impulsive

make poor choices

a pillock.

I do it for the plot.

For the secret cameras that follow me everywhere.

#11 SIT BONES, PLURAL

Yoga Loft.

PILLOCK: Yoga for beginners my arse

or sit bones

that's what downward-facing-Diane would call it

sit bones

plural.

Why can't she just say arse?

Cos it is an arse isn't it?

If she called it an arse

and every other part yano their actual names

then maybe I'd know what the fuck she was talking about.

It's an arse, Diane.

A bloody arse.

Arse.

She speaks in this

low

and

airy

voice

which she's definitely putting on

cos nobody fucking speaks like that.

They'd already started when I walked in

nicked a pair of shorts I found on the side

so fucking tight

so fucking hot

I'm scared my balls might turn into diamonds.

Diane

downward-facing-Diane

checks her watch and gives me a look.

She's a small

super-toned

gammon coloured

woman

she didn't say anything like

she just glared

the sort of look that was like halfway between how my parents looked

when I told him I was gay

and how they looked when I told him I wanted to be an actor.

Thorny subject.

I try to pretend not to clock HMV guy

he's three yummy mummies away

but then I panic that he's going to clock that I'm pretending
not to clock him

rather than actually not clocking him

so I decide to clock him to be safe

he's already clocking me

our eyes lock

time stops

he smiles

that smile

I melt like a Ferrero Rocher on a radiator.

Then we're moving

showtime.

Music.

I salutate to the sun like I've never salutated before

my cat is practically meowing

my cow is pretty much mooing

I'm warrior one

I'm warrior two

I'm warrior fucking-three

A little plank here

A little lunge there

HMV guy's

thighs

are

bulging

Mr Muscle

Mr Yoga-going-man, you

I want to sink my teeth into 'em

Not in like a Hannibal Lecter way

but in an erotic Edward Cullen sorta way

I have no fucking clue what's going on

or if I'm doing any of it right

but I'm doing it

huffing and puffing like the big bad wolf on speed.

Inhale.

Exhale.

Hug the ribs.

Inhale.

Exhale.

Chin to chest.

Inhale.

Exhale.

Fingers Interlaced.

Inhale.

Exhale.

Heart open.

Inhale.

Exhale.

Exhale.

Exhale.

Exhale.

The channel opens.

An energy block is released.

He breaks down.

It stops as quickly as it started.

End of scene.

Cut the light.

Fade to black.

#12 BRAIN FART

PILLOCK: A generation defining artist according to The Guardian

found his Wikipedia

he has a fucking Wikipedia

*had a fucking Wikipedia.

Wait

where was I

Do you know on Come Dine with Me

when they ratch through each others drawers

to try and get to know each other better?

no

too soon

I missed a bit

I missed a lot

sorry

pillock

erm.

Where were we?

#13 LEG IT MATE

PILLOCK: I'm bombing it down the street

letting everyone see what I'm going through

it was weird

the tears were weird

they came without trying

A phone call.

It's Mam.

Why does she always calls at the worst?

I'm not going there

no fucking way

pretending everything is OK

when it's not

telling each other we're fine

even though we're not

it's not

we're not

hey

are you OK?

I turn.

It's him.

HMV guy.

He looks even better this close

like those people who look better in photos than they do in person

but he's the opposite.

Erm yeah I'm

I mean

I feel like a right pillock

but

I'm fine

what happened back there

it's completely normal.

Yoga releases emotions by breaking up what I like to call

energy

blocks

he does this thing where he

pauses

on

words

like he's really tasting 'em

sucking the sugar off a tangfastic.

These energy blocks often stem from

traumas

and

memories

we've suppressed over time

he sounds like a Mumnsnet thread

you sound like a Mumsnet thread

he doesn't laugh

and I can't decide whether he has no sense of humour

or is just American

so I just say

sick.

Eugene

by the way.

American?

Colorado.

Sick

the teeth should have been give away.

Are you a Tory?

Don't know where that came from

I thought I'd thought it

turns out I'd said it.

What?

Just with a name like Eugene

I assumed

pretty liberal actually

Eugene was my father's name

from the Greek name Eugenios means

good

genes

I do a bit about only having one pair of good jeans

Levis 511s

doesn't even smirk

come on

that was fucking hilarious

nothing

So I just say

sick

I keep saying sick

Then we stand in silence for a bit.

They stand in silence for a bit.

Well thanks for coming out mate

I'll let you get back to your

to up there.

Take care of yourself.

Then he looks at me

like really looks

like he's known me for a lifetime

he's glowing

like Mary from one of 'em RE books in school

I'm painting him a halo with me eyes

when

hey

do you fancy coming back to mine?

The breeze catches his vest

I catch a peak at his

what I believe the youth of today call

cum

gutters

I'm instantly hard

erm

yeah

I do

fancy

coming.

To yours

coming to yours.

#14 ANY NEWS?

PILLOCK: Hi Carl

It's just me

Jay.

Remember me?

Your client.

Haven't heard from you in a while

so just wanted to check everything's alright

any leads

anything I can do

call me back

yeah?

#15 MOJO DOJO CASA HOUSE

PILLOCK: It's fucking massive

his house

his

mojo dojo casa house.

Y'know the sort of place that looks like it owns a Hotel
Chocolat Velvetiser?

His leccy bill must be huage.

There's these big fuck off noisy gates

electric

definitely a tory.

I don't own a bath

don't really like em anywez

but I bet he has bath

he definitely owns a bath

probably multiple baths

baths with 'em like fancy jacuzzi jets and that too

probably even one of those arse wash things that you get on
holiday

yeah.

He opens the front door

holds it open

and

gestures into the hall

feels weirdly formal

am I here for a job interview

or to fuck?

Paintings of naked men

sculptures

an ugly black vase

he's colour-coded his bookshelf

bellend

and I really want to screw it all up

y'know

swap a yellow with a blue

or a green with a pink

like when you see a trifle and you just wanna stick your elbow
in it?

Right?

Yeah.

He tells me he'll

be back

and to

make yourself comfortable

so I assume he's going to douche

that's code

innit?

They never show that bit in porn

do they?

BRB love gonna go wash the shit out my arsehole.

I look through the piccy frames and the

trinkets slash crap slash trinkets

on the mantlepiece

his parents

a brass pig

blonde guy on a beach

a clock with 'em roman numberals on it

I don't really feel time

it just sort of passes me by

sometimes at dangerous speeds

so I don't know how long I've been playing with the brass pig

when

follow me

he smiles again

solid-gum-to-tooth ratio

and everything inside me moves.

He leads me to the kitchen

naughty

when

fuck

what?

Shakshouka

which

from the two bowls on the table

I assume is a food

and not some new experimental sex position

unexpected

wrong end of the

I thought

not what I

What's a pillock?

He looks me dead in the eye when he speaks

which is kinda scary

so I start edging my egg with my fork

erm

sorry what did you say?

A pillock.

You said it earlier.

What is it?

More eye contact.

I thought everyone knew what a pillock was

never heard of it

It's like

erm

a donnat

an idiot

someone who fucks everything up

a

dumbass?

I suppose

yeah

my Dad used to call me it

stills calls me it

right

like when I drop a mug from my hand

cos I forget to hold it

or when I snapped the wing mirror off his car with the
wheelie bin

when I got excluded for setting Shannon McNeil's hair on fire
in food tec

and he smiles

laughs even

finally.

I taste the eggy tomato thing and it's alright like

but there's definitely cheese in it cos I have to hold in a fart.

Turns out we don't shag at all

which is sweet

he's really sweet

normal.

He takes my number and we hug before I leave

I can't remember that last time I actually hugged someone

The weight of my body on his feels nice

like he's taking care of me or summat

like I should feel safe with him.

I'm barely out the front door when

New message.

Eugene.

(*reading*) The word pillock

pillocks (plural)

has Scandinavian origins

and comes from the old English word

pillicock

meaning penis.

Followed by...

See you at yoga, pillock.

You can keep the shorts by the way.

They suit you.

Shit.

#16 YOGA

PILLOCK: Get into the habit of landing here in the moment.

Japanese porn is really long for some reason.

Let the mere act of showing up to to guide you from

moment to moment.

And wow it's got really good production values

and a storyline

and that

Japanese porn that is.

Allow yourself to open a new door.

A new window.

Invite to yourself to be open to the present.

After you wank do you have ever have an intense urge to

listen to music

just me?

#17 A ROUTINE

PILLOCK: It's hard

yoga.

And my cock

whenever I'm around Eugene.

I don't get what Diane

downward-facing-Diane

Is asking me to do like most of the time

I'm constantly exhaling when she wants me to inhale

and I'm not even convinced I have a core

but it certainly ain't engaged.

She wants me to find an inner stillness

well

my

inners

are never still Diane

ta very much

constant fucking chatter

it just takes time.

Beat.

If it weren't for Eugene I'd of probably given up by now

but there's summat about him that makes anything feel possible.

Turns out Salutation Sally

who I like to imagine is Diane's arch nemesis

does a class on Mondays before sunrise

we go to that too which is a miracle for me really

cos I love sleep and hate people.

We build a routine.

Me and Eugene.

Every Tuesday and Thursday.

A routine.

#18 PAPER MÂCHÉ FANNY

PILLOCK: Smolensky Gallery

a date

cos I've never been to an exhibition

a proper date.

It's like being trapped in some strange fucking coma

the sound of dying whales

stones tied to twigs

and fannies made out of paper mâché.

I'd probably think it was good

if I wasn't such a poor thick piece of shit

but it somehow just makes me pissed off

makes me want to

down nine pints of Stella

buy a XL Bully

and rip that paper fucking mâché fanny off the fucking wall.

I get a genetic gushy feeling that I don't quite belong here.

Turns out Eugene is an art curator

opening a big job next month called

Elegies: Futures Past

sounds like a shit Marvel film.

The way he talks about his work turns me on a bit

y'know 'em people you meet who have just got it

well he's got it.

Normally I have to stop myself interrupting

or trying to finish someone else's sentences

but I can't with him anywez

cos he uses words I don't even know

like

big words

he knows 'em

words

ephemeral

perspicacious

and

afrofuturism

I just smile and hope he isn't asking me a question.

He makes me

he makes me want to know more

y'know

he makes me want to be better

for him

like to buy a shumper

and maybe even

so you're an actor

right?

I hold my breath and wait for the inevitable question

anything I'd of seen you in?

Honestly.

No.

But I don't say that

I can't say that

I tell him I mostly work in film

which is jokes

cos the closest I've been to working in film is that trial shift I
did at the Odeon

where one of my calls got recorded for training purposes.

Do you know when you like someone so you lie to impress?

#19 MEAT

PILLOCK: His fridge is full of the shit that only tastes class

past the age of 25

like olives

and asparagus

cos turns out he's a vegetarian

which I wish he'd told me when we'd first met

cos he may as well be a Nazi.

He's got a load of awards on the wall up the stairs

I run my fingers in the grooves as I pass

Peter Fennell.

There's two bathrooms

but I only find one bath

it is a corner though to be fair to him

could fit my entire flat in it

there's no arse sink

disappointing.

But

he's got two toothbrushes on the windowsill

oh

and Eugene has never been to a Nandos

which is a red flag if I've ever heard one

also never tried a Twiglet

apparently you can't buy em in America

and Schitts Creek

he likes the episode where Moria does the fruit wine commercial

which is really fucking weird cos that's my favourite too

maybe I do believe in the universe after all.

Mam calls again.

Eating less meat is the equivalent of taking eight million cars off the road

you should really think about cutting it out, pillock

what?

Meat.

I don't think I'm eating enough

I wink

he turns his back.

#20 BUM FUN

PILLOCK: Do you think he's repulsed by my body?
Like we've shared a bed a few times and
you'd think
he'd of at least put his dick in my gob by now.
Like it's not like I'm obsessed with sex or anything
I just can't stop thinking about it
with him
that feeling of someone wanting you
your body.
We haven't even discussed who likes what bits where
like what category of bum fun is he?
Is he the the toast or is he the toaster?
Maybe he doesn't even like bread at all
and who the fuck is Peter Fennell?

#21 KETTY BRAIN FART

PILLOCK: I lost my virginity on ket
"want some ket"
he said
I think his name was Jack
Maybe Liam
I said OK.
K.
Not saying I encourage that sort of thing
but maybe that will get Eugene in the mood

some ket

wait

no

pillock.

Do you know on Come Dine With Me when

sorry

don't jump ahead

what was I talking about?

#22 A GUT FEELING

PILLOCK: Trust your gut

that's what google sez

which is hard for me cos mine can't even handle a Muller
Corner.

The voices in my head go back and fourth

and fourth and back

but summat still feels off

and I haven't had dairy since the sharksusanskeys.

I'm sat in his kitchen

well my body is in the room

my brain is underwater

What's up, pillock?

He drags me from the waves too fast

it takes me a minute to work out where we left off

and what the hell is going on

pillock?

He calls me that now

pillock

but in a nice way

a kind way

not like Dad.

My head is

screaming

but I can't find the words

the words

they won't

erm

do you

OK

if you

eh

alright

OK

OK

OK.

If you could

did you

if you knew that

toothbrush

wait

so

if you

I don't quite follow.

Do you like bread?

Sorry?

Like are you the toast

toaster

maybe both

or do you just not like bread at all?

What?

Is that why we haven't fucked yet

cos you don't like bread?

What are you talking about?

Is that why haven't we had the sex yet?

Are you even single?

Or do you have a boyfriend?

Are you cheating on him right now?

Or are you in like an open thing?

Woah

stop.

And I want to

I want to stop

but now I'm thinking faster than he's speaking

got to get it out

get the voices out before I

calm down

cos that's cool if

if you're open.

I'm not judging you

actually I am judging you

and actually it's not cool

cos I just thought we had

I thought we were

and that's not really my

does my body make you feel sick

make you bowk?

What?

And who's Peter Fennell?

The awards on the stairs

is he?

He's your boyfriend isn't he.

He sez nothing

then looks at me

and I think maybe for a moment I've gotten everything wrong

that I've felt too much again

that I've

over thought

over analysed

over reacted

done that thing where I subconsciously create my own reality

based on the little and

extreme

things that zipety zap through my brain

and take my interpretation of it

which is often way off

and obsessively try to analyse it

fix it

but then he sez

my husband.

Peter Fennel

is my husband.

A moment.

Right.

My ears do that weird silent thing

like when the bomb goes off in Oppenheimer.

He takes the photo of the blonde guy from the mantlepiece

hands him to me

he died nine months ago

a stroke

eighteen days after the wedding

I haven't had the heart to get rid of any of his stuff yet.

He starts to cry

I don't want him to cry

I want it to stop

but I feel too much

the feeling is too big

I didn't even get to say goodbye.

I hear too much of everything except from him

the whistle of the windows

the electricity in the walls

the drip of the tap on the bath

I want to stop the world.

Stop the feeling.

#23 YOGA

PILLOCK: Gently deepen your breath

do you think he's changed his bedsheets since Peter?

Allow any tension or stress that you've brought to the mat

to simply slip away.

Have I slept on Peter's side of the bed?

You can always come back to it later

creating some nice

fresh

new

open space.

Get fucked Diane.

#24 THE BIG ROMANTIC GESTURE

PILLOCK: The big romantic gesture

usually takes place in the final act of the film

an ultimate declaration of love

like in Big Fish

when he buys her a shit-ton of daffodils

I've always loved daffodils

they're my favourite

my nan would nick 'em from the park

and have 'em in her kitchen every Easter.

It arrives

gold envelope.

You are warmly invited to the the opening and reception of

Elegies: Futures Past

in honour of Peter Fennell

and a photo of him

Peter

he's far better looking than me.

Sick.

#25 BRAIN FART

PILLOCK: Peter Fennel

found his Wikipedia

he has a fucking Wikipedia

*had a fucking Wikipedia

a generation defining artist according to The Guardian

a pioneer in found object sculpture

so basically random shite glued to other random shite.

How did he do it?

The success and that.

Everyone loved him

and I can't help but think why him and not me.

I miss

I miss that feeling that my life would lead somewhere.

Do you know on Come Dine with Me

when they ratch through each others drawers

to try and get to know each other better?

Well

I

ADHD shutdown.

Overwhelmed.

The final lap sound from Mario slurs in his head.

#26 MUGGLE JOB, TAKE THREE

The lights flicker on.

Painfully bright.

The hum.

AUTOMATED V/O: Please enter the room.

PILLOCK: I deleted 'the app' and everything.

I'd be mad to give up on what me and Eugene have

for a bit of bussy

(whatever that actually is).

I think things are going well

well apart from the sex bit

but he wants to take it slow

there's no rush

right?

And this is what I wanted

not just sex

this is what will make this one different

make this one last

oh

I have just found out he has a husband

a dead one

don't worry

he's definitely dead

keeps the urn on the desk by the front door

do you know like when your Mam leaves Celebrations out at
Christmas for visitors?

I thought it was a vase.

He didn't mention him at first

but I get it

that's not an easy thing to tell someone is it?

And like he has invited me to the opening of his exhibition

Elegies: Futures Past

so I guess that's his way of

telling me he's taking us

seriously

so I'm dead excited.

Cos we'll get to be a real couple y'know

for people to see and that

my shot at the sort of love people snog in the rain to

like in the Notebook.

And in any of those films there's usually another man

right?

Clasabanca.

Bridget Jones.

The Worst Person in the World.

What would you do?

Like

what would you do if you were in my situation?

What was that?

Oh.

Oooops

sorry

it's diabetes

fainted on my way to big tesco

so

do you know what a bussy is?

AUTOMATED V/O: Move on to the next station

#27 BAAAA

PILLOCK: Do you know in Cumbria gay men
are outnumbered by sheep?

An awkward silence.

Waiting for the transition sound.

No that's it

that's the thought

yeah.

#28 PUSH AND PULL

PILLOCK: **If you were dandelion why would you be**
that one there
third from the right
with the wonky stem?

We're sat by the canal

and he's asking me dumb fucking questions

like

If you were a body of water

what would you be?

Apparently you can tell a lot from a person

depending on what they choose.

I say a lake

like back

home

do you go home often

the question takes me back

cos I haven't been home in years

and even then

where is home

like Cumbria is where I grew up and that

but it's hard to call the place that chewed you up and spat you
out home.

I still speak to my sisters sometimes

married

mortgages

sprogs

so they've got the spot in the centre

then there's me

on the edge

trying to keep my head above water

(shitting up my guts cos I ate a cheese string)

and it's not even like cos it's a gay thing

cos whether I came out to 'em or not

there's still a space that's always been there.

I've never really fitted in
never really fitted in anywhere
and
maybe that's what I've been trying to do
find the place where I belong
find home.
I don't know why I'm telling him this
or how we even got onto it
but his eyes meet mine
and he flashes his mush
that smile
solid gum-to-tooth ratio
and he's looking at me like he understands
and I know in that moment that he does
and that he feels the same.
I don't know much about communication styles
but whatever they are
I think we've got the same one.
He tells me that he'd be an ocean

rhythmic

constant

back and forth

push

and

pull

I wouldn't mind a bit of push and pull with him
just waiting for the tide to come in

peter was an ocean too

sorry

what was that?

#29 UGLY DUCKLING TRANSFORMATION

PILLOCK: His type must be blondes.

It's OK to have a type.

Everyone has a type.

Summat they're into.

It's OK

to

have

a

type.

I'm waiting for a parcel

so naturally my body won't let me do anything until it arrives

I track every scan

refresh the page.

Missed call from Mam.

My ugly duckling transformation

like in The Breakfast Club

or Miss Congeniality.

Blonde

I've always wanted to try it.

#30 JUST ME

PILLOCK: Hi Carl.

It's just me

again.

It's just me.

#31 YOGA

PILLOCK: Exhale

take as many steps at you need to get there.

I think about every time I've ever had sex.

Relax the shoulders.

I think about having sex with Eugene.

Chair pose.

I think about drugs

and I think about everything I've ever done wrong.

Fingers to the sky.

I think about Peter.

Right arm back.

I think about Eugene having sex with Peter.

Left arm forward.

Open twist.

Inhale.

Did I tell you that in Cumbria gay men are outnumbered by sheep?

#32 A WEEKEND AWAY ON TUESDAY

PILLOCK: We're going away for the weekend on Tuesday

let's get out of the city

it'll do us good to get some fresh air

books us some fancy hotel in Llandudno

he's paying

obviously.

Sez to meet him at his for 1pm

so I resist lying down cos if I lie down it's over.

Can't be late.

Get there for 12:45

which is a first for me cos the only thing I've ever been on
time for is puberty

I was the first lad in my year to grow a pube

used to show it off in the changing rooms

felt like a god.

You're late.

What?

I'm early

fifteen minutes early.

I said 11am.

Pillock.

You know sometimes I feel like you never really hear me

that you don't actually care

never paying attention.

It's at this point we should really chat about my ADHD and
that

but we're making real progress

and I'm scared it'll take us back to where we started

that he'll think I'm damaged

or lazy

a pillock

and actually mean it when he sez it.

Either that or he'll lie and tell me it's a superpower

which it's not

is it?

Spider Man would be a pretty shit film if instead of shooting
webs

he starts new tasks before finishing old ones

sorry Mary Jane I wanted to save you but I decided to take up
fencing.

So I don't tell him

I can't tell him

instead I just say

sorry.

Get in the car.

Pillock.

I'll do this next bit fast like one of 'em montages in Hot Fuzz.

#33 MONTAGE 1

PILLOCK: Lardedah restaurant

vegetarian

cos I'm veggie now

apparently I'm

not very adventurous

when it comes to food and I should

really

look at

expanding your culinary horizons

but I did actually try a vegan sausage roll last week

so he can shove that up his culinary horizons.

I pick the only thing I can pronounce on the menu

green

bean

salad

he knows all the names of the wines

and sez 'em in the accent and everything.

He asks me try some furry thick vegetable shite

take a bite

I don't want to take a bite

take a bite

it'll be good for you

I don't want to take a bite

it's Peter's favourite

I take a bite.

It feels like I'm chewing on a sock

it's so fucking spicy

so fucking hot

I think I can see in to my next life

I hope I win a BAFTA.

#34 MONTAGE 2

PILLOCK: Beach

under the stars

and he wants to play

guess that tune

I sing a fabulous rendition of Nothing Compare 2 U

Sinead O'Connor

we laugh

he smiles

that smile

solid gum-to-tooth ratio

it's perfect

like that film

what's it called

From Here to Eternity

From

Here

to

Eternity.

#35 MONTAGE 3

PILLOCK: I put the tap on so it sounds like I'm taking a slash

light a cig

he doesn't like it when I smoke

so I've made a habit of keeping a secret stash in my back
pocket

and a pack of chuddy.

He's only looking out for me.

With each inhale happiness feels closer

feels real

as real as the niccie rushing through my veins.

#36 MONTAGE 4

PILLOCK:

Slow

quick quick?

dancing

on the balcony

he teaches me

how to box step

how to rumba

I'm shite

but he doesn't mind

I put my hand

on his waist

he puts his hand

on top of mine

bodies so close

we might finally

#37 THAT'S A WRAP

PILLOCK: Car back

something has came up with the exhibition

can't it wait

afraid it can't

then he pulls over at the side of the road suddenly

what the fuck are you doing

gets out and starts picking

daffodils

pillock

they're Peter's favourite

I tell him

I hate daffodils

always thought they smelt of piss

he places the 'em in the footwell

my side

a question pings inside me
have you ever tried ket?
I press my heel into the petals.

#38 MUGGLE JOB, TAKE FOUR

The lights flicker on.

Painfully bright.

The hum.

AUTOMATED V/O: Please enter the room.

PILLOCK: Wilson Nixon.

Here for my prostate examination.

GMC Number 2298-summat-summat 6 puts on his gloves

tick

lubes his finger

big tick

slides said finger into the prostate simulator

looks for anything lumpy

looks for anything hard

big dick

tick

His phone rings.

Mam.

It knocks him.

I wonder if Eugene has a big...

AUTOMATED V/O: Move on to the next station.

#39 THE POSH KIND

PILLOCK: I only own one suit

bought it for my nans funeral last year

I spend a half hour trying to make myself look decent

but I end up looking #fireemoji

you look like you're going to a funeral

well it's the only one I have

I've laid something out for you on the bed

a navy suit

the posh kind

with the two sets of buttons and that

it's a little too big

a little too familiar

but if it makes him happy

you look perfect

his words like a cuppa soup on a rainy day.

His eyes get all damp

so I hold him close

the weight of his body on mine feels nice

like I'm taking care of him or summat

like he should feel safe with me.

I clock the vase

the urn

on the desk over his shoulder

watching over us.

We're going to be late.

What's it gonna take for you to kiss me?

Do you have the keys?

Yep.

I do.

Erm

they were just in my hand.

#40 BRAIN FART

PILLOCK: Do you know on Come Dine with Me

when they ratch through each others drawers to

Shrek 2!

That's what I was going to buy at HMV the day I met Eugene

the best animated film ever made

maybe even the best film ever made full stop

#41 ELEGIES: FUTURES PAST

PILLOCK: I'm nervous

I'm really fucking nervous

like when I stole that Zovirax from Superdrug but worse.

The doors swing open

the grand entrance

it's heaving

I cling to Eugene

people everywhere that all look the same

the clothes

the hair

the tilt of the head

like they were all made from the same mould or summat

murmuring

nodding

scared to make noise

like they're all in on some big secret that I'll never understand.

The champagne is free

so naturally I treat it like chips at an all-you-can-eat buffet

I've barely finished one glass when I'm reaching for another

maybe slow down on the champagne

pillock

it's important we get this right

He whirls me round from guest to guest like I'm sort of a
masterpiece

And the best part?

I don't even have to try

a wink

a smirk

and they're all enchanted.

Then Eugene's gone

among the head tilters

and the silence that's too loud

like it's pressing down on me

amplifying every thought in my head.

I can hear my own heartbeat.

Do they hear it too?

My glass gets refilled.

and I shuffle from latex gloves in concrete

to

the baby Annabel tied to scaffolding

I move and pause in designated six second intervals

six

what the fuck is this meant to be

five

I hear Peter's voice

four

you don't get this

three

well you wouldn't

two

I really need a piss

one

reach for another drink.

Applause.

Thank you.

Thank you all for being here tonight. It is a real honour to see so many faces,

familiar and new, gathered to celebrate the work of a remarkable artist and an even

more remarkable person

Peter Fennell.

Peter had a unique gift. He could see the beauty in what others often discard. A reflection of his ability to transform the ordinary into the sublime, a dialogue between the forgotten past and a hopeful future.

Elegies: Futures Past.

Peter was not just an artist.

He was my best friend

my husband

my soulmate.

I

I miss him

every single day.

He can't continue.

The first and final solo exhibition of

Peter Fennell.

He clocks me

I'm already clocking him

our eyes lock

time stops

he smiles

that smile

solid-gum-to-tooth ratio

and for the first time I feel love

his love for Peter

the sort of love people shout out in auditoriums for

like in Moulin Rouge

and I realise

that I could never compete

a love so complete

so consuming.

I reach for my secret stash of cigs

And as I grab 'em

pull 'em out

a single piece of confetti

falls

from the pocket

floats

to the floor.

I get that feeling in my gut again

like when you have a custard donut at your nans cos one won't
hurt

right

but it does

it always does

and in the moment I know

I think I've always known

Please join me in raising a glass to Peter Fennell.

What the fuck am I doing?

I thought I thought but turns out I'd said it

Everyone turns.

A little bit of wee comes out.

#42 BRAIN FART

PILLOCK: So y'know on Come Dine with Me

when they ratch through each

others

He's uncertain.

(*to the gallery*) Is it now?

Should I to do it now?

Sick.

And back.

Do you know on Come Dine with Me

when they ratch through each others drawers

to try and get to know each other better?

Well I did that

When we got back from Llandudno.

I know it was wrong like

but I thought it might help me know

know the man who came before me

know the man he loves so much.

I found their wedding video.

The minute Eugene was asleep

I'm pressing play on the remote.

It's a little grainy

and even though I could just about make out their faces

it didn't take Steven Speilberg to know

how much they adore each other.

I study it

how Eugene moves

how Peter breaths

watch 'em kissing under an ocean of confetti

almost slow motion

navy suit

the posh kind with two sets of buttons and that

their picture postcard romance

their Big Fat Greek Wedding

if either of 'em were greek.

It's perfect

they're perfect

and I want it

I want it for myself.

#43 THIS IS WHAT YOU WANTED

PILLOCK: **Quite the night, huh?**

we're barely in the door he pours himself a glass of red

I'd offer you one but I think you've had enough

I need to ask you summat

We couldn't have asked for a better turnout

and minus your little

outburst

it was everything Peter dreamed of

about the suit

it's his

isn't it?

He chugs back a slug of wine and it trickles out the sides.

Am I wearing

is this Peter's suit?

Can this wait until tomorrow?

Tonight was

a lot.

But I need to hear him say it.

Why am I wearing Peter's suit?

It's just a suit.

I watched the wedding video.

I know it's Peters.

Have you been going through my things?

You know what

I can't do this right now.

Sometimes my body does the thing where it's in motion

before I can even think about it.

I grab the urn from the desk.

Cos I'm impulsive

make poor choices

a pillock.

Why am I wearing Peter's suit?

put him down

before you do something you'll regret.

Not till you tell me the truth.

Tonight is about Peter

not about

answer the question.

Why am I wearing his fucking suit?

Or I'll

OK.

OK.

I

I don't

I don't know

Beat.

I wanted to say goodbye

what by parading me around in this clothes like

like I'm some fucking understudy

no

it's not like that at all

then what is it like?

I

maybe

I thought

I *thought*

it would be a fitting tribute.

What the fuck?

It's

symbolic

the ever presence of Peter in our lives

It's beautiful.

Can't you see that?

And for a moment I almost believe him.

I

I just wanted

I needed

to feel close to him again.

Close to him?

Or close to me?

You have no idea what it's like to lose someone

you thought you'd spend your life with

Close to him?

Or close to me?

Close to

anyone.

Anyone who could...

You were just

there.

So all of this

all of this was just

Put him down.

Did you ever want me?

Did you ever want me for me?

I've tried

but how could I…

You don't even know who you are.

You're

a pillock

a donnat

a dumbass?

Busting my gut to be a little more Peter

a little more ocean a little less lake maybe

chipping away the little parts of myself I have left

hoping

dreaming

that you would see this spark that lives inside me

that it would ignite

burst into tiny fucking stars

and it could be enough to fill that space inside you

and that you'd know

everyone would know

that I'm worth summat

see me for who I

for what I

I wanted you to want me so fucking bad

I would have

I wore his fucking suit

Beat.

I WENT TO FUCKING YOGA.

Beat.

but I'll never be enough for you

will I?

Beat.

Hand him over and I'll explain.

I'll explain

everything.

OK.

And I go to

I go

to give him the urn

hands shaking

fingers trembling

but

Smash.

A whirlwind of black

Peter clouds the room

my toes go sweaty

then silence.

Then silence.

You fucking pillock

he sez it in a way I've never heard him say it before

like Dad

you fucking pillock

just like Dad

sorry

I'm sorry I'm sorry I'm sorry

I didn't mean

Confetti from the suit pockets becomes ash.

he grabs me by the chin

I try to push him back

but his lips are on mine

sweet yet with the sting of shiraz

and we're kissing

bodies so fiercely mashed

glued

together

pulls me the ground

he's strong

Mr Muscle

Mr Yoga-going-man you

fragments of the urn crunch into my side

blood merging with ash

ash merging with blood.

He smears his husband across my body

my chest

my face

my lips

undoes my belt.

Inhale.

Exhale.

Hug the ribs.

Inhale.

Exhale.

Chin to chest.

Inhale.

Exhale.

Fingers Interlaced.

Inhale.

Exhale.

Heart open.

Inhale.

Exhale.

And whilst the thing he's doing with his tongue feels fucking
class

I realise

I'm so fucking lonely

I'm game to let someone do whatever they want to me

so I can feel wanted for a moment

to pretend I'm not alone.

I want you

to get off.

I slither along the floor

towards the door

there's blood

eye contact

I take one last look

like really look

goodbye Eugene.

He grabs my leg

but I boot it out behind me

claw the handle

and then I run

I have no clue where I'm going

know the roads

or which one leads where

and the gash in my side sends larl ripples of pain down my leg

but I run

away from the chaos

completely

completely

alone

I run

so the chaos can't find me.

Maybe they were right putting love in the films

maybe it can't live anywhere else for me.

And he's right y'know

I have no fucking idea who I am

still working out who to be

how to be

And yeah I might be a

pillock

but you know what?

"Blessed are the forgetful

for they get the better even of their blunders"

Eternal Sunshine of the Spotless Mind.

Oh

and it is big by the way

his penis.

#44 YOGA

PILLOCK:

Draw your shoulder blades together and rise up strong.

Like the powerful being that you are.

Bring your hands in to centre.

If you pray

you can pray here.

If you don't

maybe just whisper quietly to yourself

I love you.

Namaste.

#45 THE BIG BREAK

He sits in the audition waiting room.

He fumbles with his script.

He stands and sits a few times.

Bites the skin round his fingers.

His phone rings.

He hesitates.

He answers.

PILLOCK:

Hi Mam.

How are you?

Good

how's Dad?

Good

I'm fine

yeah

I'm fine

yeah.

Actually

no.

I'm not.

I'm not fine Mam.

I can't really talk right now.

I'm waiting to go in.

An audition.

Aye

so turns out my agents not dead and just a lazy bastard

yeah.

But

but maybe I could

I could

drive back

home

at the weekend.

We could all go for a walk or summat

talk.

Yeah.

Bassenthwaite

like we used to.

Ice-cream?

I can't eat dairy Mam.

Oh

really?

Do they

are they doing that now?

Aye

raspberry ripple.

A VOICE: Jay Parker.

PILLOCK: I've got to go, Mam.

The first time he's heard her say it.

I love you too.

Bye.

He puts the phone down.

A VOICE: Ready?

PILLOCK: Sorry.

                 Could I just have a minute please?

                          Thanks.

He breathes.

Closes his eyes.

Tries to stop the voices. Calm the chaos.

                          Hello.

                           I'm

                       My name is

                       Jay Parker.

        I'll be reading for the role of homosexual number three.

An inhale of breath.

Blackout.

THE END

ALSO AVAILABLE FROM SALAMANDER STREET

I LOST MY VIRGINITY TO CHOPIN'S NOCTURNE IN B-FLAT MINOR by Sebastian Gardner
ISBN: 9781914228162

A bittersweet comedy which focuses on the disparity between classes and how much of your self identity you would comprise for someone you love.

STEVE AND TOBIAS VERSUS DEATH
by Sebastian Gardner & Daniel Kettle
ISBN: 9781914228872

This throat-ripping zombie comedy pits the gore of horror against the hysterical instability of family life.

ALGORITHMS by Sadie Clark
ISBN: 9781738429394

A bisexual Bridget Jones for the online generation.

CANDY
by Tim Fraser
ISBN: 9781914228834

Comedy-drama about identity, masculinity, mental health and, most importantly, love.

COWBOYS AND LESBIANS by Billie Esplen
ISBN: 9781914228902

Charming, queer romantic comedy about British schoolfriends writing a parody American coming-of-age romance.

IF YOU LOVE ME THIS MIGHT HURT
by Matty May
ISBN: 9781914228513

An uncensored and funny show about rage, suicide and so-called self-care... all through a queer lens.

Printed in the USA
CPSIA information can be obtained
at www.ICGtesting.com
LVHW021125210924
791748LV00001B/89